Blue Bottle Mystery

Blue Bottle Mystery

An Asperger Adventure

Kathy Hoopmann

Jessica Kingsley Publishers
London and Philadelphia

First published in the United Kingdom in 2001 by
Jessica Kingsley Publishers Ltd,
116 Pentonville Road,
London N1 9JB,
England
and
325 Chestnut Street,
Philadelphia, PA 19106, USA.

www.jkp.com

Library of Congress Cataloging in Publication Data
A CIP catalog record for this book is available from the Library of Congress

British Library Cataloguing in Publication Data
A CIP catalogue record for this book is available from the British Library

ISBN 1 85302 978 5

Printed and Bound in Great Britain by
Athenaeum Press, Gateshead, Tyne and Wear

Contents

To Karl

Chapter 1

Miss Browning-Lever

"Ben, stop that!"

Ben froze. Stop what? He was tilted back in his chair with the front legs off the floor. Slowly he leaned forward and let the legs touch down.

Across the room, Miss Browning-Lever still frowned. So that was not why she had yelled at him. He sat up straighter and stopped swinging his legs. No, wrong again. Miss Browning-Lever came towards him, angry, scowling. Why was she always hard to understand? Why was he always in trouble? He hated school!

"Get your pen out of your mouth," Andy hissed. Andy was Ben's best friend. They had been together since preschool. Five years was a long time to be mates.

Ben took the pen out just before Miss Browning-Lever got to his side. He flapped his hands nervously out of sight under the desk. He always flapped when he felt nervous, but Miss Browning-Lever didn't approve.

"I've told you a hundred times to keep that pen out of your mouth, Ben. If you swallow the lid, you'll choke," she snapped.

"It's not a pen, it's a texta," Ben pointed out.

"Are you trying to be smart with me, young man?" She spoke close to his face, loudly.

Ben hesitated. He *was* smart. He was so far above his class in maths and science that he helped the year sevens with their homework. Teachers called on him to help work the computers and he was the school chess champion. But then he remembered, 'trying to be smart' meant being cheeky.

"No," he answered, looking down.

"No, *what*, and look at me when you speak to me," Miss Browning-Lever yelled. A bit of spit sprayed his face. Ben flinched. Spit meant germs.

What did she want him to say? Ben took a guess. "No, um, I'm not being smart," he said, still not lifting his eyes to meet hers.

"No. I'm not being smart, *what*! Mr Jones."

The class was silent. Their teacher had been in a bad mood all day, even more so than usual. Andy thought she must have fought with her boyfriend, but no one believed him. Miss Browning-Lever was too cranky to have a boyfriend. Everyone had been trying to stay out of her way, but Ben always seemed to annoy her.

"Listen, son," Miss Browning-Lever said with a hard voice, "I'm sick of your attitude. When you speak to me, you will address me as Miss Browning-Lever, understand?"

Ben felt sick. What did 'address her' mean? He didn't understand any of this conversation. He didn't know why he was in trouble. How he hated school!

"No," he managed to say the word without crying, just.

Miss Browning-Lever looked at him as if he had gone mad.

"No," she repeated in astonishment, "No? No what, Ben? What are you saying 'no' to?

No, you won't say my name when you speak to me?"

"Ah," Ben breathed a sigh of understanding. That's what she meant! She wanted him to say her name. He hated her stupid name anyway and could never say it right. Mr Bell, the headmaster suggested that they call her just Miss Lever, but she snapped, "My name is Miss Browning-Lever and that is what the children will call me." Ben avoided saying her name ever since. Wriggling in his chair, he could see his shoe sticking out from one side of the desk. He felt like his shoelace, twisted round and round and tied in a knot.

Suddenly Miss Browning-Lever stood tall. "This is the last straw. Get out of here, Ben," she snarled, "I am so sick of your behaviour. Out. Now!" She pointed to the door.

Ben shuffled out from his desk and stood up, his head bowed low looking at the floor. Where was the last straw she talked about? What did it have to do with anything? He went to the troughs at the side of the room and turned on the water.

The class gasped. What was he doing?

Miss Browning-Lever went crazy. "What the hell do you think you are doing, Ben?" she shouted. The rest of the class gaped at each in amazement. The teacher said "hell." Wasn't that a swear word?

Ben froze again. Finally he got the nerve to reply, "I'm washing my face. You spat on it."

Miss Browning-Lever went purple in the face. She smashed her hand down on his desk so hard that it snapped his ruler. "Get out!" she screamed.

Ben stared at the broken ruler, horror on his face. "You broke my ruler," he said as he began to cry. He swallowed hard, his face screwing up into an ugly, blubbering mess. Coming back to his desk, ignoring how close he was to his furious teacher, he picked up his ruler. It was as clean as the day he got it six months ago. His name that had been neatly written on one side was shattered along the JO of Jones. In a sudden rage he kicked over his desk, scattering his book tray everywhere. Girls screamed and the boys yelled and Miss Browning-Lever turned in a barely controlled fury and snatched up the phone from the wall and called the headmaster.

Ben didn't hear what she said. He was too busy trampling his ruined ruler into a thousand pieces; his hands flapping wildly, two out of control propellers.

Chapter 2
The Playground

"What did Mr Bell say?" Andy asked. He took a bun out of his lunchbox and bit into it.

"I've got to pick up all the papers round the little kids playground and then apologise to the teacher," Ben grumbled.

He took his sandwich out of the plastic wrap and looked at it in disgust. Cheese. He always had peanut butter. *Always.* Then he remembered. Grandma told him that they'd run out of peanut butter that morning. Ben's mother died when he was little, so each morning his Dad dropped him off at Grandma's on his way to his job. Dad was the local handyman so every day he did something different. Each afternoon, Ben went back to Grandma's place until his Dad could pick him up again. Ben hoped Grandma would go shopping today and get more peanut butter. He tossed the cheese sandwich in the bin and peeled open his banana. At least he got that. A banana for lunch was the first thing that had gone right all day.

"Aw, bad luck about picking up papers and I can't help you either," Andy said. "The basketball try-outs are today. I want to get on the team. At least you don't have to go to that." Ben hated basketball and most other sports, and Andy knew it.

"Yeah, that's good," Ben agreed, "and I don't mind picking up papers on my own." Andy knew that too. Ever since preschool, Ben enjoyed searching at the base of shrubs and behind walls to find tiny bits of rubbish. The little kids' area would be spotless by the end of play time.

"I don't want to say sorry though," Ben said. "*She* broke *my* ruler and she doesn't have to say sorry to me."

"Teachers are always right, Ben." Andy wiped the blobs of cream from around his mouth, missing bits, smearing others.

"No they're not. She spelt computer byte with an 'i' yesterday," Ben pointed out.

"No, I didn't mean that," Andy smiled. Ben always believed exactly what he heard. Last week when the music teacher said, "Jump to it," Ben actually jumped on the spot.

"I mean that they think they are right and there's nothing we can do about it. We're kids, remember."

"Well, it's still not fair," grumbled Ben.

"That's life!" Andy said as he bounded to his feet ready for basketball. He walked his friend as far as the playground, then he waved and ran down to the courts to join a large group around the sports teacher. Andy was one of the smallest kids there. He didn't have much chance of joining the team, but he was always ready to give things a go.

Ben turned to the playground. It was a mess. There were papers everywhere, but that was fine. Ben knew that time went faster the more mess there was to clean. He picked up a paper bag, one someone's lunch had come in, and began to stuff other papers into it. There was a simple beauty to picking up rubbish. Ben thought about the playground and in his mind he divided it into four large squares. He cleaned each square completely before moving to the next. The garden bed areas in the back corner behind the swings were his favourite. You were only allowed to walk beyond the cement edges up into the shrubs and flowers if you were picking up rubbish. In the very back corner, the bushes had overgrown and tucked behind them was a small clearing where you could be completely hidden from everyone. But Ben always picked up all the papers in the squares first and left the corner 'til last. It was something special worth waiting for. He did that when he ate too. The boring, yukky food first, the best left 'til last. There was a pattern to it that pleased him.

"Whatcha doing, Jones."

Ben looked up and saw Troy and Scot, a couple of rough kids from Miss Black's class next door.

"Picking up papers," Ben said, avoiding their gaze.

"So we've been a naughty boy, have we?" Troy pushed him gently on the shoulder. Ben hated to be touched and Troy knew it. Ben tried to ignore the push and thought about Troy's words. "So *we've* been a naughty boy" …did that mean Troy was in trouble too?

Troy pushed him again. "What, not talking to me today, Jones. Now that's not very polite, is it?"

Ben tried to remember the bullying steps they were taught over and over again. First, ignore the bully. If that doesn't work, tell the bully to stop.

"Stop it, Troy, leave me alone," Ben tried to walk away but Scot was too quick. He tripped Ben, giving him a hard shove at the same time. Ben fell over the cement edging into the flowers that had been recently watered. He got mud all over his hands and on his shirt. He hated being dirty! With a roar he got up and flew at Scot and Troy, but the two boys skipped away out of reach. They danced around the enraged Ben, kicking the rubbish that had spilt from the paper bag. A large group of kids watched, laughing at Ben's fury.

"Hey, teacher coming!" Troy suddenly called and the two boys ran off to the oval laughing, knowing they wouldn't be found amongst all the kids down there. The rest of the crowd vanished and Ben was left alone. He sobbed with anger and frustration, feelings he didn't know how to describe in words, let alone name. He bent down to pick up all the papers again when he found himself looking at a teacher's red high heeled shoe. Not Miss Browning-Lever! Anyone but her! Slowly, he looked up and saw his teacher leaning over him.

"Are you all right, Ben?" she asked softly.

"Yeah," Ben said getting up, sniffing and wiping his nose on the back of his hand. Miss Browning-Lever handed him a pink tissue and he took it, blew his nose hard and then he stuffed the tissue into his rubbish bag.

"Did they hurt you?" she said. "I saw Troy and Scot pushing you around. They think they got away, but I'll speak to them after lunch."

Ben looked up in surprise. Why was she being so nice all of a sudden? Then he saw that Miss Browning-Lever's eyes were puffy and red and her face had been recently washed and was still a little wet.

"Have you been crying?" Ben asked curiously. "I didn't know teachers cry."

"Ben," Miss Browning-Lever said slowly, "I want to say that I'm sorry I yelled at you and that I broke your ruler. You're a good kid really, and I know I've been cranky lately, it's just that…oh well, never mind. I bought this for you." She handed Ben a brand new ruler with his name neatly printed on the side, then she turned and walked away.

Ben watched her go, confused. Now what was he supposed to do? He never knew how to handle things that he hadn't come across before. Andy would have known whether to chase after the teacher and say thank you or creep away and hope she forgot about you. Life was so confusing sometimes. Most of the time actually.

With a sigh he put the ruler down his shirt to keep it clean and went back to picking up papers, faster now. He wanted time in the back corner, away from everyone. Time to think. It didn't occur to him to leave the papers and go there straight away. He still had two more grid squares to clean.

Chapter 3

The Blue Bottle

Andy found Ben in the hidden corner about ten minutes later.

"I didn't get in the team," he said. "The coach took one look at how short I was and said I had to grow a bit first. The other kids told me to ping off."

"What does ping off mean?" Ben said, imagining somcone walking along saying 'Ping, ping, ping'. He was never afraid to ask Andy to explain things he didn't understand.

"You know," Andy said, "Get lost. Go away."

"Uh, OK," Ben said.

"That's life," Andy shrugged. "Next year maybe."

The boys sat in silence, digging holes in the dirt with sticks. Andy's hole was deep and messy. Ben's hole was a neat circle. Finally Ben pulled the new ruler out of his shirt. "Look," he said, "The teacher gave it to me."

"Miss Browning-Lever? You're joking!" Andy cried in amazement.

"No, I'm not. It's true," Ben assured him.

"Man, you must have given her some apology."

"I never said sorry at all. *She* said sorry to *me*."

"Really?" Andy cried.

"Yeah. And her face was wet. I think she'd been crying. Why would she do that? I've never seen a teacher cry before."

Andy grunted, "You weren't in Troy's class last year when we had that relief teacher for a week. Troy had her in tears, twice!" He handed the ruler back to Ben.

"Troy and Scot pushed me over." He showed Andy his dirty hands. "Why do they always pick on me? I never hurt them." Ben kept working on his hole.

"That's life. Scot and Troy pick on everyone," Andy said.

"Do you think there could be a blue bottle in this garden?" Ben said suddenly.

"What?" Andy looked at Ben in surprise. If there was one thing about Ben that even Andy could not get used to, it was his sudden changes of conversation. It was as if sometimes Ben held half a conversation on his own before he said anything aloud.

"Do you think there could be a blue bottle in this garden?" Ben repeated.

"A blue bottle, one of those stingers in the sea?" Andy had no idea what Ben was talking about.

"No, a blue bottle." Ben pointed to his neat hole in the dirt. At the bottom was the curved base of a bottle made of blue glass.

"Oh, *that* sort of blue bottle." Andy leaned closer. "Keep digging. Let's see if we can get it out."

Together the boys scraped the dirt away.

"I think it's a vase of some sort," Andy said shortly. "It's got silver rings around it."

It wasn't big and it didn't take long to dig out. Ben held it up to the light and brushed off the extra dirt. It was about the size of his hand, with a wide base that thinned to a long neck. It was completely undamaged and even had a cork plugged into the top.

Ben pulled out the cork and a puff of white smoke sprayed into the air. He tipped the vase upside down but nothing came out.

"Empty," he said. "It's pretty. Maybe I'll give it to the teacher."

"To Miss Browning-Lever? Why?" Andy snorted, "After the way she treated you this morning."

Ben shrugged. "She's upset about something. Grandma said tears mean someone's sad."

"Everyone knows that," Andy said.

"Well, I don't have a mother remember. Grandma has to teach me. Anyway I wish Miss Browning-Lever was happy and didn't cry any more. Maybe this vase would made her happy."

Andy took it and peered at it closely. "It looks really old, and it's heavy. It's probably worth a fair bit. Hey!" he cried as he thought of a great idea, "Maybe it's a genie's bottle and we just helped it escape from thousands of years trapped under the ground."

"Yeah!" Ben giggled at the thought. "Maybe we've got three wishes. I wish for heaps and heaps of money."

"And I wish I was really tall and that I had huge muscles and that the coach would beg me to come on the basketball team," Andy grinned at the thought.

"And I want all the computers in the whole world." Everyone knew Ben loved computers.

"And I want a million more wishes," Andy cried.

"And I want Scot and Troy to blow up and burst everywhere," Ben gloated.

"And I wish there was no school ever again," Andy added in glee.

"Me too!"

Then the bell rang. The boys looked at each other sadly.

"I guess we don't get our wishes then," Andy said, and shrugged. "That's life."

"Yeah," said Ben standing up and brushing the dirt from his clothes. "That's life."

Chapter 4

Friday Night

The next day was Friday and both Andy and Miss Browning-Lever were away. The relief teacher was all right though. She was kept busy trying to stop a couple of the girls from fighting all day and she had no time for the quiet boy in the back row. Even lunchtime was fine. Scot and Troy were on detention and no one else bothered Ben as he wandered round searching for tiny stones that got lifted up from the concrete in the assembly area.

"Do you want to go out for pizza?" Ben's Dad asked when he picked him up from Grandma's that night.

"No thanks," Ben said. When Dad said pizza, he meant that he'd eat the pizza and he'd buy Ben fish and chips. Ben liked plain food. He hated it when food was mushed up together on top of a pizza. But even the thought of fish and chips wasn't enough to make him want to stand in line for ages with heaps of people he didn't know. Not today. All he wanted to do was go home, where everything was the same and nobody gave him a hard time or spoke to him with big words he didn't understand.

His Dad looked at him sideways as drove the four wheel drive out of Grandma's driveway. It had 'Jack Jones for Jobs' written in black on the side with a picture of a wheelbarrow and rake.

"Hard week?" Dad asked.

"It was OK," Ben said. He always said that. It was easier than trying to explain things. "I got some stones today." He took a handful out of his pocket and showed them to his father.

"You didn't spend all lunch picking up stones again, did you?" Dad said with a slight frown.

"Yeah. I like picking up stones."

"What about playing a game of soccer occasionally? Doing what the other boys do?"

"I don't enjoy those games, Dad. I'm not a soccer kid," Ben said.

"It's good for you. Running around, getting some exercise."

"I'd rather pick up stones."

Dad frowned but didn't say any more.

"Listen mate," Dad said after a while, "I know tomorrow's Saturday and I usually stay home with you, but I've got a rush job on. It'll take most of the morning. Will you be all right with Grandma?"

"OK," Ben said happily. Grandma had an old computer which couldn't even take CDs but there were a few games on it that Ben enjoyed. She also had a wonderful garden that he was allowed to weed. It was quiet at Grandma's.

"Some lady called up desperate today," Dad explained. "Her mother just died and the funeral is on Monday. She was expecting visitors from all over the place and her yard's a mess."

"OK," Ben said. "How did her mother die?"

"I don't know. It's not the sort of thing you ask a stranger."

"OK." Ben was silent all the way home. As they drove into their garage, Ben said, "Now she's like me."

"What?" his Dad asked.

"She's like me?"

"Who's like you?"

"That lady you said, whose mother died. We're the same. We both don't have a mother."

Dad stopped the car and looked at his son. "Yeah, mate," he said patting him roughly on the shoulder. "But don't forget. You've always got me and Grandma."

Ben nodded, "OK."

Dad cooked some sausages and put them on rolls with tomato sauce. They ate on the deck looking over the back garden. It was a bit over-grown. Dad spent all day cleaning other people's back yards. He didn't want to do more gardening when he got home. Ben loved Friday nights. Dad believed that Friday night was a time for relaxing. On Fridays they sat on the covered deck to eat, even when it was raining. They always ate something easy, or had a take away. Dad drank a beer and Ben had a coke. During the week, Ben went to bed at eight thirty. On Fridays, he and Dad watched the gold lotto draw together, and then he was allowed to stay up until nine thirty. It was a lovely set routine and it never changed. Ben felt comfortable when things were the same.

"Did you put our lotto in today, Dad?" Ben asked.

"Of course," Dad replied. "Which numbers did you choose this time? I didn't look."

Dad always let Ben choose the numbers.

"I made up a new pattern. I got your's, mine and Mum's birthday dates and the birthday months and squared them then divided them by pi 'til I got a number on the form. I didn't put in the decimal points though."

"Trust you to do that. You divided them by pi, did you," Dad laughed. "You mean, pi, the area of a circle thingy?"

"Yeah."

"Clever kid," Dad said smiling. "Well, with a bit of pi on our form we're sure to win tonight."

Ben stacked the dishwasher, which wasn't very full, but it was better than washing up. He then went and played on the computer until Dad told him the lotto draw was starting.

Sitting with his pencil ready, he waited for the numbers to be called. Suddenly a tiny swirling white cloud spun in front of the TV. What was it? But as soon as it had come, it vanished and Ben forgot about it as the balls began to fall from the barrel. When the last one fell, the pretty girl on the screen said, "Well, those are our numbers for tonight, 26, 31, 6, 19, 5, 34, and the supplementary number is number 9. Good night everyone and I hope all your dreams come true." She smiled and waved. The ads started and Dad looked across at Ben.

"No luck, mate?"

Ben didn't move.

"Ben?" Dad asked again. "How did we go?"

Ben didn't say anything. He gave Dad the form, then stood up and began jumping up and down flapping his hands in a frenzy.

Dad looked at the form in amazement. Their numbers had been crossed off.

They had just won lotto!

Chapter 5

What To Buy

It took until Sunday to find out how much lotto money they had won. They sat Grandma down before telling her.

"Six hundred thousand dollars!" Grandma cried, sinking back into her chair. "Oh my goodness, Jack," she said, "What are you going to do with all that money?"

"It will be hard, but we'll think of something," Dad smiled.

"It won't be hard, Dad. We've already made a list each," Ben said.

"It was a joke, Ben" Dad smiled again.

"Oh, OK."

"So what's on your list, Ben," Grandma asked. "What do you want to do with all that money?"

"Well, first I want a new computer with the biggest memory I can find, and I want the internet, then I want to buy you a computer too, maybe even with a modem and a laser printer, and then I'll get some new tools for your garden and a sprinkler system so you don't have to water all the time. Dad could put it in for you."

Grandma smiled. "You're a good kid, Ben." She turned to her son. "And you Jack, what's on your list?"

"Well, I'll pay off the loans on the house and four wheel drive. I also want a new ride-on mower, then I'll be looking around for a new house. With a pool probably. One big enough for you to come and live with us if you want. Or I'll buy you your own new house if you'd rather."

"Oh, Jack, what a lovely thought, but I don't want to leave here," Grandma said, "This is my home. If you're feeling really generous you could buy me a new TV, my old one's almost had it, but I'm happy just the way I am."

"Dad," Ben said, "What do you mean we'll buy a new house? I don't want a new house. I like our old house."

"Come on, mate. Think about it. You could have a brand new room, new bed, your old one's falling apart, plus the new computer you want can go in its own computer room. You could swim everyday in your new pool. Heck, I could even afford to send you to that flash private school on the hill. How'd that be, Ben?"

Ben started to flap his hands.

"No new house, Dad. No new school. No new bed." His flapping grew stronger. The thought of all those changes was too much.

"Stop flapping, Ben," Dad said angrily. "You know I hate it when you do that."

Ben flapped harder. His head nodded furiously.

"What's wrong with you kid? Any normal boy would love all those things. Why can't you be normal for a change?" Dad shouted.

Ben started to cry. The flapping was frantic now.

"Jack," Grandma put her hand gently on her son's arm. "Let me deal with this."

"Oh for goodness sakes," Dad yelled, "What a lot of fuss about nothing. It's about time the kid grew up, that's all."

"Jack," Grandma said again. "I'll handle this. Why don't you go for a drive for a while?"

Dad looked from Grandma to Ben, who was completely out of control by now, yelling and flapping as hard as he could. To Jack, Ben looked stupid. Without saying a word, Jack stormed from the room, slamming the door behind him.

Grandma let Ben cry and flap until he quietened to a hiccupping sniff. Then she sat him down next to her and put her arm gently around his shoulders.

"This is hard for you, isn't it," she said softly.

Ben nodded.

"You're feeling confused and a bit scared about all those things Dad wants to do, aren't you?"

Ben nodded again, still sniffing. Grandma gave him her tiny lace hanky, and he blew his nose hard.

"Things are often difficult for you to understand, I know that, Ben, but you have to try to think of how your Dad's feeling too. He only wants those things to make you happy, you know that, don't you?

"Yes," Ben whispered.

"Well then, you let me speak to him and we'll work things out, and in the mean time, don't be sad and angry. Your father loves you very much."

"I found a blue bottle, Grandma."

Grandma blinked. She didn't understand how Ben changed topics so quickly, but she was used to it.

"Did you?" she said. "Tell me about it."

When Dad came back an hour later, Grandma sent Ben out to pick some cherry tomatoes. He enjoyed that job, but the vines were almost empty and it didn't take long to gather the last few ripe ones and put them in a container.

As he came back into the house he heared Dad and Grandma talking.

"Ben doesn't need a doctor, Mum," Dad said. "He needs a good spanking, if you ask me."

Ben couldn't hear what Grandma said, but then his Dad yelled, "Well, you organize it then. At least I've got money to waste now, which is just as well, those shrinks cost a fortune."

Ben came in with the tomatoes in his hand. "What's a shrink?" he asked.

Dad and Grandma looked at each other then Dad looked away and Grandma said, "Ben, your Dad and I have been talking. We think that maybe a special doctor could help you not be so upset about things. Maybe he could help you to understand other people a bit more. Would that be all right?"

Ben thought about it. Could a doctor really help him? It would be good not to be so different any more. But then the thought of going somewhere new, to a person he didn't know, frightened him.

"No thanks. I don't want to," he said finally.

"But it could help you, Ben. And I'll be there with you," Grandma said gently.

Ben hesitated. "Maybe, one day," he said and Grandma smiled.

Chapter 6

Growing Up

The next day at school Ben ran up to Andy, a big smile all over his face. "I've got to tell you something," he said in a loud whisper, "but it's a secret." Dad said not to say anything about winning the money yet, but it was too exciting not to tell Andy. "Come on."

"What is it?" Andy yelled as Ben took off, running to their private place behind the shrubs. He knew it was out of bounds, but nowhere else was safe enough. Only when they were hidden from everyone's view did Ben tell his secret.

"Guess what!" he said in his loudest whisper. "We won lotto! Six hundred thousand dollars!"

Andy sat there with his mouth wide open. Finally he squawked, "Six hundred thousand dollars! You're a millionaire!"

"No," Ben corrected him, "Six hundred thousand dollars is not a million dollars. It's only zero point six of a million."

"You're rich!"

"Yeah. Isn't it great. I'll get you a present. What do you want?" Ben asked

"A super Nintendo! Mum said I can't have one 'cause they cost too much. Would you get me one?"

"Sure," Ben said easily.

"What are you going to do with all that money?" Andy asked.

"I want a new computer with the internet and a modem and email and a laser printer. Dad wants to get a new house, but I don't want to."

"Why not? It'd be great. I'd love a new house."

"Dad says he wants one with a pool," Ben said.

"A pool! Wow! We could swim all day!" Andy cried in excitement.

"Maybe," Ben said, beginning to realise that buying a new house might not be all bad.

"Dad also wants to send me to some doctors that cost a lot," he told his friend.

"Send you to some doctors? Why? Are you sick?" Andy asked.

"I don't think so. I don't know."

"I went to a doctor on Friday. That's why I was away from school," Andy said. "I've got aches in my legs and arms. The doctor said it was growing pains. You know how I had to go to the doctor two weeks ago for that sore throat?"

Ben nodded.

"Well, I've grown three centimetres since then! The doctor couldn't believe it."

Ben looked at Andy. He still seemed the same height to him. Andy usually came up to his shoulder. "Stand up," Andy demanded, "and I'll show you."

Ben and Andy stood side by side. Andy was now just a little higher than he had been last week.

Ben shrugged. "Maybe you could go on the basketball team now?"

"Nah, I've got to be taller than this."

Suddenly a spiral of smoke twisted in front of the boys. They watched it in fascination.

"What's that?" Andy asked.

"Don't know, but I've seen it before," Ben replied trying to remember where that had been.

"So have I," Andy cried. "At the doctor's. I pointed it out to Mum, but she couldn't see it."

"It's strange." Ben reached out to touch it, but it suddenly disappeared.

Just then the bell rang and the boys ran to class. When they got there, Mr Bell informed everyone that Miss Browning-Lever would be away from school for the whole week. The relief teacher was a cheerful man called Mr Smith. Ben loved his name, it was so easy to say, and he was funny too. He told lots of jokes, some of them Ben even understood without Andy explaining them to him, and he made everyone laugh a lot.

By lunch time, Ben and Andy had forgotten all about the mysterious smoke.

Chapter 7

The Wisp

The week passed quickly. Mr Smith was a funny teacher, but he made them work hard, and before Ben knew it, Friday came round again. Andy had been away from school that Thursday, but on Friday morning he limped into the grounds obviously in pain.

"Why are you walking like that?" Ben asked, meeting him at the gate.

"I'm growing more," Andy answered, rubbing his legs as he sat down on a nearby bench seat. "Mum took me to the doctor's again yesterday and I'm another three centimetres taller than last week. The doctor said he's never seen anyone grow so fast. The trouble is, I ache all over. It's horrible."

"Stand up," Ben ordered, "Let's measure each other."

The boys stood side by side and Andy was now the same height as Ben.

Ben nodded wisely. "You'll be on the basketball team soon," he said.

"I won't be on any team if I hurt this much all the time," he groaned sitting back down. "Hey, I just remembered something. When I was at the doctor's I saw that smoke again, you know that swirly fog stuff. Mum couldn't see it though. It's really strange."

"Yeah," Ben said, thinking about it. "What could it be?"

"Who knows? Maybe we should get our eyes checked."

"What does that mean?" Ben asked, imagining criss-cross patterns on his eyelids.

"You know, go to an eye doctor to see if our eyes are OK."

"Nah," Ben replied. "I don't want to go to any more doctors. I went to one after school on Wednesday with Dad and Grandma. He asked me lots of dumb questions and made me take my shirt off. I hated it."

"My doctor does that too," Andy said.

"Dad and Grandma have to go back and see him without me tomorrow. Grandma said she'd ring your Mum to see if I can stay with you."

"That'd be great!"

"And then," Ben continued, "Dad said he'd take us to Sizzlers at night. But I don't want to go."

"Not go to Sizzlers! You're crazy! I'd love to go. I thought you liked Sizzlers any way."

"Yeah, I do," Ben said, "But Dad wants to bring a lady with him. I don't know her. He tidied her garden because her mother died...."

"Like you," Andy said.

"Yeah, like me, but Dad went to school with her years ago and she looked sad, so he said he would take her to Sizzlers."

"Great!"

"It's not great," Ben said. "I hate new people." He flapped his hands gently.

"Look," Andy cried suddenly, "It's that smoke again!"

Ben jumped up and down in excitement, flapping harder. "What do you think it is?" he called loudly.

Several other kids came over. "What are you looking at?" one girl asked staring around in puzzlement.

"The smoke!" Andy yelled jumping onto the seat trying to grab it as it floated gently past him.

Ben tried to grab it too, but it rose higher out of their reach.

"I can't see anything," another kid said.

"There!" Ben pointed as he ran backwards and forwards his head rolled back, watching the smoke bob about above him.

"There's nothing there," the girl said. "You guys are weird." She and her friends walked away, shaking their heads and twisting their fingers in a spiral close to their ears. Crazy boys!

Ben danced on the spot in excitement, flapping madly. Andy jumped from seat to seat trying to grab the white puff above him. Then as quickly as it came, it disappeared.

"Something really funny is going on here," Andy said, still standing on the bench searching for the smoke. "How come we're the only ones who see it?"

"Did you know that Grandma's computer only has 200 megabytes," Ben called to his friend.

Andy looked at him in bewilderment. "What are you talking about?"

"Grandma's computer, the 486 sx 33 only has zero point two gigabytes," Ben said.

"The 486 what? No, don't tell me," Andy put his hands up to stop Ben from talking. "Ben," he said slowly, "We were just chasing some smoke that only we could see and it disappeared without a trace, and you start talking about computers? You *are* strange."

"Ah, sorry," Ben said automatically. He was used to apologising to people. "Can I tell you now?"

"No!" Andy shouted walking away stiffly.

Why did Andy do that? Why was he angry? Ben found it so hard to understand people sometimes. He watched his friend walk away, then went up to the girls who were chatting amongst themselves. He said, "Grandma's computer has 200 megabytes."

"Get lost, Jones," one of the girls cried angrily. "We were talking before you rudely interrupted us."

"Ah, sorry," he said, then slowly, feeling hurt, but not knowing why, he went to his special place behind the shrubs. He started to dig in a neat circle again, remembering the blue bottle he found the last time he dug there. Something was tickling at his memory. Something to do with the smoke. Then it came to him. The first time he had seen the white puff, it had come from the blue bottle!

He jumped up in excitement, and bumped his head on a jagged branch above him. Ignoring the pain, pain never worried him much anyway, he ran across the oval to the basketball courts where Andy was shooting baskets.

"Andy!" he yelled, "Andy, I know what the smoke is! It's a genie from the vase!!!"

Chapter 8

Which Wishes?

"Do you think it's possible? Could it really be a genie's bottle?" Andy said, hoping it was true.

Earlier, the two boys sneaked into their class-room and took the vase from Miss Browning-Lever's desk. She had left it there from the week before and a dead flower sagged limply over the lip. With a bit of searching, Ben found the tiny cork and the two boys now sat behind the shrubs.

"It must be true," Ben said holding the bottle to the light, trying to look inside. "Think about it. Do you remember that I wished for heaps and heaps of money? And then we won lotto!"

"And I wished I was really tall and that I had huge muscles. And now I'm growing so fast the doctor can't understand it," Andy grinned. "It must be a genie's bottle!"

"And that smoke stuff we keep seeing must be the genie!" Ben yelled in excitement.

"Shhh," Andy hushed his friend. "Someone will hear us."

"What else did we wish?" Ben asked his friend with a voice just a tiny bit softer. He found it hard to talk quietly.

The two boys thought for a while.

"Didn't you want all the computers in the world?" Andy asked.

"Yeah, that's right, and you wanted lots more wishes. Hey, I wonder if we got those? We could have anything we wanted for the rest of our lives!" Ben shouted happily.

"Shhhhh!" Andy whispered.

"But which wishes did we say first? Don't we get only three?" Ben said.

"That's only in fairy books. Maybe this genie gave us all our wishes," Andy said hopefully.

"Well, let's try," Ben suggested. "Wish for something right now. If we get it we'll know we have as many wishes as we want."

Andy thought hard then said, "I wish for a double chocolate swirl ice cream!"

Nothing happened.

"Maybe it doesn't happen straight away. I had to wait 'til night time to win lotto," Ben pointed out.

"Well, you try," Andy said.

Ben thought a moment then said, "I wish I had twenty computers right now!"

Nothing happened.

"Why did you wish that?" Andy complained. "They're hardly going to fall in your lap are they?"

"Computers are great," Ben defended himself. "Did you know......?"

"I don't want to know anything about computers, OK!" Andy cried. "Let's think about our wishes. If the one about a million more wishes didn't come true, then what else did we want?"

Suddenly, Ben looked at his friend his mouth open in horrified excitement, "I remember, we wanted Scot and Troy to blow up and burst everywhere!"

"Man!" Andy gasped, "Is that possible?!"

"I don't know, but if it did we could go to prison for killing them!"

"No we couldn't!" Andy insisted. "We haven't done anything wrong. If they did blow up it would be nothing to do with us."

"But we wished it! It would be our fault!" Ben was upset now. Scot and Troy were horrible, but he didn't really want them blown up.

"Maybe we should try to unwish it," Andy suggested. "You know, make another wish saying that the wish that we wished isn't what we wish any more."

Ben said nothing. He was trying to understand what his friend just said.

Andy grabbed the bottle, pulled out the cork and called down into the neck. "Hey genie! We don't want Troy and Scot to blow up, OK."

Ben suddenly choked, "I remember another wish! We said we didn't want there to be school ever again! How will that happen? Could the school blow up too?!"

Andy grinned at the thought. "That wouldn't be so bad. Maybe we could leave that wish there."

"No way!" Ben cried. "Then Dad would send me to that private school on the hill. Besides, someone might get hurt. This is scary, Andy. What if all our wishes really truly come true?" He grabbed the bottle and yelled into it. "Hey genie! Don't blow the school up or hurt anyone, OK." He turned to Andy. "Do you think that'll stop it?"

"Don't know," Andy replied.

Suddenly the two boys looked in amazement as the white wisp of smoke spun before them. It floated in the air for a few seconds then disappeared.

"Do you think it heard us?" Andy whispered, staring at the spot it had been.

"Yeah, I think it did," Ben whispered back quietly for once.

"I hope I still get taller though, and get my big muscles," Andy said.

"And I've already won lotto."

"I wonder what the third thing was, if wishes really come in threes."

"Can't remember," Ben sighed, "but maybe we stopped it in time."

"Maybe," Andy agreed.

Chapter 9

Asperger Syndrome

That Saturday afternoon, Dad and Grandma dropped Ben off at Andy's house and went to visit the doctor on their own. They had to wait a long time in the waiting room and Dad was already cranky when he finally sat in the doctor's office.

What he heard next didn't make him any happier.

"Asperger Syndrome! What on earth is Asperger? It sounds like a vegetable," Dad snapped at the doctor.

Grandma gave him a look to tell him to behave.

"It's caused by a problem in the brain. It makes people think and act differently from others," the doctor explained as nicely as he could, scratching at his beard as he spoke.

Dad grunted, "Well, that's Ben all right. He certainly thinks differently from me…and everyone else," he added.

"Exactly. People with Asperger's have problems with relating to others. They find it hard to understand what other people are thinking or feeling. And it is hard for them to say what *they* are thinking or feeling. When they explain things to you they may leave important bits out. Often they find something that really interests them and they become little geniuses in that area and will tell you about that topic over and over and over again."

"Computers!" Grandma and Dad yelled together.

"Exactly!" the doctor agreed. "Asperger children usually hate large groups like in organized sport, especially team sports."

Dad nodded sadly. "I'd love him to play soccer, but he's not interested."

"Think of it this way, Mr Jones," the doctor explained. "Imagine if you couldn't kick a ball very well, and you were put into the middle of a group of kids who yelled at you, called you names and rushed around so you forgot who was where. Imagine you couldn't remember who was on which team anyway because they changed every day. How would you feel?"

"Terrible," Dad admitted.

"That's how life is for Ben every day. Full of rules he doesn't understand, people with moods he doesn't understand, who use language he doesn't understand. He's like a visitor on a new planet every day of his life. The fact that he has one very good friend is wonderful, because Asperger children can find it hard to make friends. They are often very lonely little people."

Dad and Grandma were quiet for a while, trying to imagine how life was for Ben.

"So how can we help him," Grandma asked finally.

"Well, unfortunately it's not something that you can cure with medicine," the doctor said, "And it's not something that he will out grow. He will always have Asperger Syndrome."

"Oh, great!" Dad sighed.

The doctor smiled sadly. "You say great, but you really mean it's *not* great. If you say that to Ben he will not understand you. People with Asperger's find it hard to understand sarcasm too."

"So what *can* we do?" Dad asked.

"You are already doing a lot of things to help without realizing it. You have let him follow his interests, you have encouraged his friendship with Andy. You try to explain things to him as much as you can when he is upset."

Dad coughed, "Well, Grandma is a lot better at that than I am," he admitted.

"But you're a good father, Mr Jones, and I can see that you love your son very much. If you try to understand how he looks at life then you'll find that it is easier to cope with his bad times as well as his good ones."

"It's not easy to understand Ben, Doctor. I try but it's not easy."

"I know, but you only have one kid that's hard to understand. Ben finds it hard to understand everybody! Here," the doctor gave Grandma and Dad lots of papers to read and the phone number of an Asperger support group. "Sometimes it helps to talk to others with children similar to yours. And don't worry too much. Everyone is a bit different in their own way. Ben is a very special child with very special talents all of his own. When you start to understand how he sees the world, you will learn that seeing things differently from others is not such a bad thing."

Dad and Grandma were very quiet in the car on their way home. Finally Dad said, "Well, you were right, Mum. He does need some help."

"I think we'll all need help for a little while, until we get used to the idea. It will be the best for him though, for us to understand Asperger's better."

"He's a pretty good kid, when you think about it," Dad said. "Imagine having to cope with everything all these years, and we didn't know."

"Yes," Grandma said. "He's a good kid. He's a very special kid."

Chapter 10

Sue

That night, Andy and Ben sat in the back of the four wheel drive on the way to pick up Dad's old school friend.

"Her name's Sue. You'll like her," Dad said as he pulled up in front of a small brick house with a neatly trimmed garden at the front. He got out and walked down the path and knocked on the door.

Ben slunk down in his seat. "I wish we could go on our own," he complained to Andy but Andy wasn't listening. He was looking out the window with his mouth wide open in surprise. "Look!" he managed to say, pointing at the house. "It's Miss Browning-Lever!" Ben peeked out wide eyed.

Miss Browning-Lever was wearing jeans and a pale blue shirt. Her hair was fluffy and loose, not tied back in her normal style. She smiled at Dad and laughed at something he said. She did not look cranky like she did at school. She looked happy and pretty.

"What will she say when she sees us?" Andy whispered. "We've got to hide!"

The two boys crouched on the floor at the back of the car hoping they could not be seen.

"Boys, get up!" Dad called as he got near to the car. Ben knew he was annoyed but didn't want to show it in front of Miss Browning-Lever. Andy got up, and Miss Browning-Lever looked at him in surprise, but Ben stayed crouched low, fluttering his fingers.

"Ben," Dad called again, "Say hello to Sue. Sue, this is my son, Ben."

Andy kicked his friend to make him obey. Slowly Ben raised his head, but looked at the floor. "Hello," he said.

Miss Browning-Lever gasped out loud. "Hello, Ben," she managed to say. "I didn't know you were Jack's son." She smiled at him nervously.

Dad looked at the two of them curiously. "Do you know each other?" he asked.

"Ben is in my class," Miss Browning-Lever replied.

"Really!" Dad said. "I never put two and two together. Come to think of it, Ben never says your name much, he just calls you 'the teacher'."

"Well, my name is a bit of a mouthful," she said with a smile.

"It's four, Dad," Ben said.

"What?" Dad looked at him confused.

"Two and two is four. Everybody knows that."

Dad sighed, "That's not what it means, son, it's…" Dad paused trying to think of an easy way to explain what he meant.

"Your Dad just didn't realize that I was your teacher, that's all," Miss Browning Lever said with a smile.

Dad gave her a relieved look.

"We're getting a new computer," Ben said, flapping his fingers, trying to keep his hands still and out of sight.

"Not now, Ben," Dad said, smiling at Sue, trying not to show his embarrassment.

"Actually," Miss Browning-Lever said, "I'm interested in computers myself. I'm getting a new one too." Dad opened the door for her and she got in and turned round to the boys at the back. "Which one do you think would be best for me?"

Dad and Andy sighed. They knew how much Ben could talk about computers, and the rest of the trip to Sizzlers was spent listening to him.

"I'll have fish and chips," Ben said when they finally got into the restaurant.

"That's a change," Dad said.

"No it's not," Ben corrected him. "I always have fish and chips."

Dad shook his head, "That's what I meant, Ben. I was joking."

"Oh, OK," Ben knew about jokes, but he didn't think that one was very funny.

"Can I have the seafood dinner?" Andy asked. "I love prawns and stuff."

"I'll have the salad bar," Miss Browning-Lever said.

"And a good old steak for me," Dad told the man behind the counter.

They found a seat near the window. The waiter bought out a plate of fried bread and they all started eating hungrily.

"So," Dad said cheerily to the boys. "Is Sue a good teacher?"

Andy smiled and said, "Yes, Mr Jones. She's great."

Ben nodded and added, "She's OK when she doesn't shout at me."

Miss Browning-Lever went bright red.

"I'm sure that doesn't happen too much," Dad joked, trying to stop Ben from talking by kicking him under the table.

"Why did you kick me, Dad?" Ben asked.

Dad started to get very embarrassed and angry, when Miss Browning-Lever put her hand gently on his arm. "It's OK, Jack. Ben is right. I have been a very cranky teacher lately, but my mother was so sick, that all I could think about was her."

She turned to the boys. "Did you know that my mother died?"

Ben nodded, "My mother's dead too," he said.

"I know." She smiled at Ben kindly.

"We're the same," he said.

"A bit the same," she agreed and then the waiter brought out the food.

The wisp of smoke swirled across the table and Andy and Ben watched it in amazement. It stopped in front of Andy and he put his hand out to touch it just as the waiter put the seafood dish in front of him. "I hope you enjoy mussels, sir," the waiter said. "There's a special on today. The seafood platter comes with an extra dish of mussels. They're good large ones too. Happy eating."

Mussels! The two boys looked at each other in surprise. Andy had wished for big muscles, like muscles on his arms, not mussels in a seafood platter! The genie got it wrong!

The puff of smoke floated up gently out of sight and Andy and Ben craned their heads to watch it go. They were sure they heard a tinkling of laughter as it disappeared.

Chapter 11

The New House

The next weekend Dad announced to Ben and Grandma, "I've got something I want to show you." He made them get into the car without telling them where they were going.

"Can't I stay home, Dad?" Ben begged. "I want to play the computer."

"You play too much computer," Dad replied.

"But the computer's fun."

"Well, I want you to come for a drive," Dad said, trying not to get annoyed.

"Where are we going?" Grandma asked.

"It's a surprise," Dad said.

Ben put his head in his lap and refused to look out the window. He waved his hands at his side like two tiny wings.

Dad shook his head in frustration. Why did Ben do that? Didn't he know how silly it looked? He was about to yell at Ben to sit up properly, when Grandma whispered, "Leave him. He'll come around."

Dad frowned, but said nothing.

They drove for about ten minutes until they got to a bushy area near the state forest. Finally Dad stopped and Ben peeked out quickly and saw trees hanging over the edge of a large wooden fence. Big trees. Trees that would be great to climb. Dad and Grandma got out of the car, but Ben put his head back on his lap and refused to move. A man came over and shook Dad's hand. He had not seen Ben in the back seat.

"Ready to see your new house, Jack?" he asked.

Ben flinched in shock. Had Dad sold their old house without telling him?!!

He flapped harder, rocking backwards and forwards, making little grunting sounds.

The man peered in the car. "Is he all right?" he asked Dad.

"Ah, no, he's not actually. Um, he's....he's sick," Dad lied. "Ah, he wants to throw up. I don't think we can stay today. Perhaps I could call you and make another time to check out the house."

"Yeah, right, mate," the man said, trying hard not to stare at Ben too much.

Dad and Grandma got back in the car as quickly as they could and they drove away very fast. Dad stopped the car as soon as they got out of sight from the man.

"What was all that about?" Dad turned around and yelled at Ben.

Ben made the silly noises even louder with his head still on his lap.

"It was too much of a surprise, Jack," Grandma said softly. "Ben needs things explained to him. I know it was a lovely thing to do, but give Ben a chance to understand what is happening."

Dad stared out the window with his arms crossed and his mouth in a hard line. "It's not *our* house anyway," he snapped. "I thought you'd like to look at it. Think about it."

"I know, Jack, but now Ben has to know it too." She got out of the car and got in next to Ben. "Ben," Grandma said gently. "Ben, can you hear me?"

Ben stopped whimpering and nodded his head.

"Dad says that he hasn't bought that house. He just wants us to look at it. If we drive past the house again, would you look out the window? We won't stop. We'll just drive past so you can see it. Would that be OK?"

Ben sniffed and nodded again. He sat up and wiped his eyes. Dad didn't say a word as he started up the car. He didn't say a word as he drove past the house once again.

"See, Ben, it's got a pool," Grandma said. "With a slippery dip on it! Wow. That would be good, wouldn't it?"

"Maybe," Ben agreed, "but I still like our house better."

"Sure you do," Grandma said.

Dad didn't say a word all the way home, but when they pulled into their drive way he managed to say. "Would it be OK if we drove past the house again tomorrow and stopped the car this time? Just to look, not to get out."

"OK," Ben said happily as he jumped out of the car. "I'm going to play the computer now."

Dad and Grandma looked at each other.

"Don't try and surprise him, Jack," Grandma said. "He needs to know what is going to happen, or he gets confused and frightened."

Dad nodded. "It's hard for me to remember that. I used to love surprises when I was his age."

"Yes, I know," Grandma smiled. "But I also seem to remember that you were hopeless at maths. In some ways it's for the best that he's different from you."

"Yeah," Dad agreed with a big sigh. "But it's still so hard to know what to do, Mum. He doesn't act like other kids."

"Be thankful for his good points. He's wonderfully clever in his own way. Just don't forget that."

Dad nodded then said, "Maybe I'll go inside and let him teach me how to use my new computer."

"Good idea," Grandma said with a grin, "You do that."

Chapter 12

The House Warming Party

The next day and the next and the next, Dad took Ben to the house. They looked at it through the car windows. They looked at the pool with the slippery dip. They looked at the huge lawn, perfect for riding bikes on. They looked at the gardens. "You could have a garden area all of your own, if you want," Dad suggested, "Grow your own flowers."

They looked at the big verandah that went as far around the house as they could see.

"Does it go the whole way round?" Ben asked.

"Ah," said Dad. "You can find out when we go inside. We could do that next Saturday?"

"OK," Ben said happily.

Dad smiled.

The next Saturday, the same man as before met them at the gate.

He looked at Ben strangely, "Feeling better, mate?"

Ben nodded, not looking him in the eye. The man opened the huge gate and they all walked inside. The first thing Ben did was run to the pool. It was fenced off to one side of the garden and he peered though the rails and stared at the beautiful curved edges surrounded by palm trees. It was much better close up than it was from the car.

"Wow," was all he could say.

The house was old, but well kept and was made of large red brown bricks and the verandah *did* go all the way round. Inside, the ceilings were high with patterned edges and enormous French doors in the family room let in light. There was no furniture, because the previous owners had already left, but thick cream curtains still hung in place giving a fresh clean feel.

"It's beautiful," Grandma said. "And it's so big, too."

"Apparently it's almost a hundred years old. It was the first house in the area. But wait until you see this," Dad said leading her through to the back yard. Ben immediately ran to a huge trampoline sitting on the lawn. "It comes with the house," Dad called to him. "The previous owners were going overseas and didn't want to take it with them."

He smiled as Ben bounded higher and higher in the sky, then he turned to Grandma, "But that's not what I wanted to show you," he said. He lead her along a covered pathway to a smaller house surrounded by flowering shrubs. "It's a granny flat," he explained. "If we buy this place, I want you to come and live with us. Ben needs you close. Do you think you could live here?"

Grandma was so happy that she started to cry, "Oh, Jack, it's lovely," she sniffed. "I'd love to live here."

They went back to Ben who was still jumping on the trampoline.

"Do you want to see the room that you could have as your bedroom?"

"No. I want to jump."

"Leave him," Grandma said. "He's happy. Don't spoil it."

It took over two months before they actually moved in. They had a huge house-warming party and invited all their friends for dinner. Ben wasn't sure how they were going to warm the house, until Grandma explained that a house-warming party was like giving the house its first birthday party. Dad fried steak and prawns on the barbecue and all the kids swam in the pool, jumped on the trampoline and played on Ben's brand new computer. Miss Browning-Lever was there too. She had spent a lot of time with them lately, something that

Ben didn't mind. She was a lot of fun when she wasn't cranky. Dad was certainly happy all the time, and since he and Grandma had explained to Ben all about Asperger Syndrome, Ben was happier too knowing that his problems had a name and that he wasn't different for no reason.

The new house even had a secret place like the playground at school, only here it was high in a tree. Andy and Ben had climbed to escape from all the other kids.

"It's a great house," Andy said watching the crowd around the pool. "I'm glad you decided to move here."

"Yeah, it's good," Ben agreed. "My computer is the best thing though. Did you know that it can......?"

"Yeah, right," Andy stopped him from saying any more. He had heard all about that computer for months now. Ben never tired of talking about it.

"I don't know how you can understand all that computer stuff. It's way too hard for me."

"My Asperger brain makes it easy," Ben said. Andy knew about Ben's Asperger Syndrome. Sometimes he wished he had Ben's brain that made maths and science and computers easy to understand.

Since Miss Browning-Lever and Mr Bell had been told of Ben's Asperger Syndrome, life at school was much better for him. Miss Browning-Lever tried hard to use simple ways to explain things, and she only set Ben one thing to do at a time, so he didn't get confused. The bullying in the playground had stopped as well, partly because Ben was taught how to deal with it, and partly because the teachers watched out for him more. To have the tallest kid in the school as his best friend helped a lot too.

"Have you stopped growing yet?" Ben asked his friend.

"I think so. I hope so," Andy replied. "It's a bit funny being the same height as the teachers, but it's great on the basketball team."

"Do you really think the genie did it?" Ben asked.

"Sure," Andy said. "Do you still think you got all this from it too?" he pointed to the house and pool below them.

"Yep," Ben replied. "No one would believe us though. It's our own secret."

"I'm glad Troy and Scot didn't burst, or the school burn down or anything yuck like that," Andy added.

"I guess, but I'm just glad they don't pick on me any more," Ben said.

"I wonder what our third wish was? I wish I could remember," Andy said then peered down between the leaves. "Look." He pointed to Ben's Dad with his arm around Miss Browning-Lever. "You might get a new mum soon. Do you think they will get married?"

Ben shrugged, "Maybe. I'm glad she's happy now. She was such a horrible teacher when she yelled all the time."

Suddenly the two boys looked at each other in surprise. "That was it!" Andy said first.

"Yeah!" Ben shouted. "I wished that she was happy just when I opened the bottle and the smoke came out! That was the first wish!"

They watched Sue as she smiled up at Dad. Dad gave her a quick kiss on the lips and Andy and Ben both groaned together. "I wish they'd stop that, though," Ben said. "Kissing's yuck. Germs!"

A puff of fluffy smoke spiralled in the air above Sue and Dad and drifted on the breeze towards the excited boys. It floated lightly before them before slowly fading away. As the boys stared at the spot it had been they heard a tiny voice on the wind cry softly, "Good bye."

One Year Later

On the day of the wedding, Andy and Ben sat in the front row of the church next to Grandma. Their friends and relatives sat in the rows behind. Only Dad and Sue were out the front at the altar. They wanted a small wedding and there were no bridesmaids or best men.

"Are you glad you've got a new mum now?" Andy whispered.

"Yeah, she's nice," Ben said too loudly and got hushed by Grandma. "But the best thing is that now she'll change her silly name. Mrs Jones sounds much better."

Andy laughed and he got hushed by Grandma too.

Then the pastor said, "I now pronounce you man and wife. You may kiss the bride!"

"Yuck!" the boys groaned, "Not again."

It was Grandma who laughed this time.

Then the pastor came forward to the rest of the church and announced, "Please stand for the newly married couple, Mr Jack Jones and Mrs Sue Browning-Lever-Jones!"

"Oh no!" Ben cried out loud. "I'll never be able to say that!"

Useful addresses

If you want to find out more about Asperger Syndrome, these organisations are a good place to start:

Autism Association Queensland Inc.
The Executive Director
PO Box 363,
Sunnybank QLD 4109
Australia
Email: mailbox@autismqld.asn.au
Tel: 617 3273 0000

**Asperger's Syndrome Support Network
(Queensland) Inc.**
PO Box 123
Lawnton QLD 4501
Australia
Email: revans@powerup.com.au
Tel: 617 3285 7001

The National Autistic Society
393 City Road
London EC1V 1NE
Tel: 020 7833 2299

Autism Society of America Inc.
7910 Woodmont Avenue, Suite 650
Bethesda
MD 20814–3015
USA
Tel: 301 657 0881

Autism Society of Canada
129 Yorkville Avenue, Suite 202
Toronto
Ontario M5R 1C4
Canada
Tel: 416 922 0302

The ASPEN (Asperger Syndrome Education Network) Society of America Inc.
PO Box 2577
Jacksonville
FL 32203–2577
USA
Tel: 904 745 6741

Asperger's Syndrome Support Network
c/o VACCA
PO Box 235
Ashburton
Victoria 3147
Australia

Autistic Association of New Zealand
PO Box 7305
Sydenham
Christchurch
New Zealand
Tel: 03 332 1038

Websites

National Autistic Society
http://www.oneworld.org/autism_uk/index.html

OASIS (Online Asperger Syndrome Information and Support)
http://www.udel.edu/bkirby/asperger/

The Centre for the Study of Autism
http://www.autism.org

Asperger's Disorder Homepage
http://www.aspergers.com